Dear Parents:

Congratulations! Your child is taking the first steps on an exciting journey. The destination? Independent reading!

STEP INTO READING® will help your child get there. The program offers five steps to reading success. Each step includes fun stories and colorful art or photographs. In addition to original fiction and books with favorite characters, there are Step into Reading Non-Fiction Readers, Phonics Readers and Boxed Sets, Sticker Readers, and Comic Readers—a complete literacy program with something to interest every child.

Learning to Read, Step by Step!

Ready to Read   Preschool–Kindergarten
• big type and easy words • rhyme and rhythm • picture clues
For children who know the alphabet and are eager to begin reading.

Reading with Help   Preschool–Grade 1
• basic vocabulary • short sentences • simple stories
For children who recognize familiar words and sound out new words with help.

Reading on Your Own   Grades 1–3
• engaging characters • easy-to-follow plots • popular topics
For children who are ready to read on their own.

Reading Paragraphs   Grades 2–3
• challenging vocabulary • short paragraphs • exciting stories
For newly independent readers who read simple sentences with confidence.

Ready for Chapters   Grades 2–4
• chapters • longer paragraphs • full-color art
For children who want to take the plunge into chapter books but still like colorful pictures.

STEP INTO READING® is designed to give every child a successful reading experience. The grade levels are only guides; children will progress through the steps at their own speed, developing confidence in their reading. The F&P Text Level on the back cover serves as another tool to help you choose the right book for your child.

Remember, a lifetime love of reading starts with a single step!

For Jesse

All rights reserved. Published in the United States by Random House Children's Books, a division of Penguin Random House LLC, New York.

Step into Reading, Random House, and the Random House colophon are registered trademarks of Penguin Random House LLC.

Visit us on the Web!
StepIntoReading.com
rhcbooks.com

Educators and librarians, for a variety of teaching tools, visit us at RHTeachersLibrarians.com

Library of Congress Cataloging-in-Publication Data is available upon request.
ISBN 978-1-5247-7191-1 (trade) — ISBN 978-1-5247-7192-8 (lib. bdg.) —
ISBN 978-1-5247-7193-5 (ebook)

Printed in the United States of America

10 9 8 7 6 5 4 3 2 1

This book has been officially leveled by using the F&P Text Level Gradient™ Leveling System.

STEP INTO READING®

2

STEP

READING WITH HELP

THE EVIL PRINCESS
vs.
THE BRAVE KNIGHT
MAKE GOOD CHOICES?

by Jennifer L. Holm and Matthew Holm

Random House New York

It is morning
in the castle.

Time to wake up!

The Brave Knight
puts on his armor.

The Evil Princess
puts on her crown.

There is cereal
and milk
for breakfast.

The Evil Princess
and the Brave Knight
want to eat
something else.

8

Their Magic Mirror

says no.

Cake for breakfast
is not a good choice.

After breakfast,
they go outside.

They play
on the swings.
It is fun at first.

But then they
get bored.

So the Brave Knight
practices jumping.

Jumping is a
good choice.

Jumping in the mud
is not.

Their Magic Mirror
tells them to
come inside.

They color pictures.

It is fun at first.
But then they
get bored.

So the Evil Princess
casts a spell.

It is not
a good choice.

They promise to try.

It is lunchtime.
There is tuna
and broccoli.

They eat it.

It is a good choice.

After lunch, it is raining.

They must play inside.

The Brave Knight
does not
swing his sword.

It is a good choice.

The Evil Princess
does not try
to turn the cat
into a dragon.

It is a good choice.

After dinner,
they do not fight
over what show
to watch.

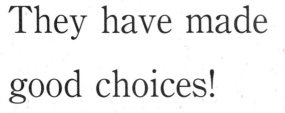

They have made
good choices!

And now it is
time for bed.

The Brave Knight
takes off his armor.

The Evil Princess
takes off her crown.

They get in bed.

They sneak down
to the kitchen.

They eat
ice cream.

And they both
agree it is
a very good choice.

So does the cat.